Wiped

BY
Madison Park

ISBN: 978-1-969181-04-7

WIPED

◊

Off in the distance, away from the crowds and the chaos, I could see the skyline of the City and the glimmer from the outline of the wall that keeps it clean. I could only see it on some days, because most days it's covered by the orange fog or the dust storms.

All the factories and mines cloud up the sky even more, making it look unbreathable. When the rain clears all the orange pollution, I can see clearly. In their City, the sky is blue and the air is clear. Even if it's fake, we are all jealous of it. The City looks pure and not so stuffy.

The nearest rainforest is so far that our water is never fresh, always out of a can. Even the buildings here are orange, rusty because they are almost never cleaned. Inside of the houses, the dust still comes in through the cracks. When there is too much dust, we have to wear masks that cover our faces, and sometimes we even have to wear them inside.

My building is made of dusty metal, and there are no windows because we are always trying to keep the air outside.

On the very few days it rains, I try to spend all of my day outside and I use a telescope to look at the City far away. One time, I saw fake snow coming out of the sky and it made the whole City sparkle. That's why I want to get a job there, so I can leave this suffocating town.

I got up from my chair and looked out at the City one last time. I always sat on my old plastic chair on the roof to look out at the City. The sky today was too polluted for me to see well, but even the slight glimpse I saw was enough to make me excited. I took the stairs down to my floor and entered my unit. The lights were still off as my whole family was still asleep. I checked the clock to make sure I had enough time before I had to get to Elizabeth's.

I put on a navy polka dot dress and chose my least damaged pair of boots. As I was tying my shoes, I heard a voice from behind me.

"You know how the selection is, it's not fair even if they say it is," my mom said, leaning against the door.

"Why are you awake? It's still early in the morning, you said you weren't feeling well."

"I couldn't fall asleep, everyone's coughing is too loud," she said, her eyebags heavy.

"I couldn't sleep either. I know it's not fair, everyone knows it. But I still have this good feeling about my selection."

"Just try not to expect much. Also, make sure to say bye to everyone before you leave. I'm pretty sure they're all awake now."

I heard light sniffling and coughing from the other rooms and walked over to my grandparents' room.

A small light was lit, and I whispered goodbye to my grandma, who was taking some small red pills. My grandpa was asleep next to her, quietly snoring. She just smiled and waved goodbye, as she had lost her voice a few days before.

I then went to my parent's room to say goodbye to my dad and my brother. When my dad saw me, he pointed at my brother who was asleep. He then quietly stepped out of the room.

"Hi, how are you feeling?" he asked, sniffling.

"Pretty good, I think it's gonna go well."

"Good, you never know what could happen, I guess. Sorry that we can't go. The city just doesn't give us enough days off, and we need the rest. We all wish we could go."

"It's ok, I'll just tell you guys how it goes."

"Okay, good luck!" he whispered.

I waved goodbye to my mom again and finished tying my shoes. I took the creaky stairs down, accidentally brushing my hand against cobwebs on the railing. I went down two floors and knocked on Elizabeth's door. She opened the door and told me to come inside quickly.

"I woke up late, and now I'm barely ready!" She said through her toothbrush.

"It's fine, you still have some time."

"We're leaving in five minutes, guys!" Shouted Elizabeth's dad from the other room.

"Okay!" Elizabeth answered, running to the bathroom.

We were getting ready to go to one of the most important events in our lifetimes. The event was called the Ceremony, but it didn't feel like a ceremony. Everyone here dreads this day as the government selection has been basically rigged ever since it was created. I didn't feel the same way, though. I didn't have that dreary feeling; I had a good feeling I was going to get a job in the City. I was helping Elizabeth pick out her shoes, and we chose the pair that was the least damaged. Most of our boots were worn out and faded from long exposure to the sand outside. I put on my jacket and laced my shoes tightly. We left the building and headed for the Ceremony right on time.

There was a bunch of foot traffic on our way as most of our streets are narrow paths, barely fitting two people side-by-side. The ground was cracked, and the strong wind blew the sand around the walls that felt like they were closing in on either side. There were uneven, dusty staircases stuck between two buildings. Everyone in the town who had recently turned 18 had to attend, no one was free from work here. Most people acted like they already knew what job they were getting, but I was expecting anything and had high hopes. Even my family didn't seem to believe me when I said I was going to get a nice job in the City. The best job that I had seen anyone get from here was a custodian at a government building in the City, and that was Elizabeth's mom. I hoped for that job as well, hearing stories from her about how clean and impressive the inside of the City buildings were.

Once we arrived, Elizabeth's dad went a separate way to take a seat in the crowd, and we went backstage. They directed us to a seat number to go sit on. Since my last name starts with S, I was in the back rows, but luckily Elizabeth was sitting right in front of me. It was sad knowing only Elizabeth's dad was waiting for us in the crowd, but I knew no one else could make it due to their health.

After being distracted by the crowd, I finally focused back when Elizabeth's row stood and lined up. I clapped for her as her name was called and she was handed a slip with her job assignment.

We weren't allowed to open it until the Ceremony was over and the curtains were closed. Once you got your assignment, you went off to the side of the stage and waited for everyone's names to be called.

My palms started sweating looking at all the empty seats in front of me. A stage director told our row to stand up and get in line as the last person in Elizabeth's row got their slip. I was one of the first people up in my row. They announced the name of the person in front of me, and he went off to the side.

"Natalie Simon," the announcer said. I heard a light round of applause from the crowd and stepped up to get my paper. People say that the more they fold your sheet, the better the job is. I looked down at my paper to see it was tightly folded into a small square. I tried to not let it get my hopes up, but I was still so excited. I went off stage to the side and stood with my group. As all the rows slowly got up and received their assignment, my palms grew super sweaty and the more I waited, the more I wanted to peek at my paper. I kept looking at Elizabeth, who looked just as nervous as I was.

The last line was called, and I watched as everyone joined us on the side of the stage. Finally, the announcer made his closing remarks and the curtains closed, leaving us free to check our papers. Me and Elizabeth went to the back, away from the crowd.

"I can't open it. I'm too nervous!" I said, gripping onto my paper.

"Me neither. Can we read each other's papers so it's easier?" Elizabeth asked.

"Okay," we exchanged papers. I looked at Elizabeth's paper, which was loosely folded into a triangular shape.

We counted to three and looked down in worry. The paper said, 'Elizabeth Perry—Factory B worker'" My jaw dropped when I saw the words. I had thought that Elizabeth might've had a good chance at a better job because of her mother, but she got the same quality job as almost everyone else in town. I looked up at Elizabeth's face, who was reading my slip. She looked up at me with a sorry look.

"Natalie, I'm sorry. You got the factory job," she said, handing me my unfolded slip.

"No way, you also got Factory B. How is this possible?" I gave her paper to her and looked furiously at my own.

'Natalie Simon—Factory B worker' was written largely on the paper in all red. I felt like screaming, but when I looked around, I saw sad expressions on everyone's faces. Elizabeth looked just as upset as I was feeling.

I frantically went around the stage, asking the others what they had gotten on their slips. When they opened their papers to show me, the same results were written on every page. Some said Factory A or L, construction site B, Landfill worker, Shipyard worker. There were some that were better than others, but I soon realized that nobody on the stage had gotten a decent job. I thought of all the times the announcers had promised 'fair and unbiased results.'

I stomped up to the announcer who was now leaving the stage.

"Yes, do you need something?" He asked, turning around.

"This can't be a fair lottery! Look at these results! You guys rig them and only say that they're fair!" I yelled, causing people nearby to stare.

"No… they're not. All assignments are final, and I would recommend you go home now,"

He turned his back and quickly marched away with his folders in hand.

I crumpled my paper into a ball and shoved it into my pocket. Elizabeth walked over next to me.

"Are you ready to go home?" she asked. When I looked around the stage, I saw that most kids were already leaving with their parents, all wearing a disappointed face.

"Yeah," I sighed.

We met with Elizabeth's dad and showed him our slips. Even though he was upset, he looked like he was expecting it. That's how I felt with everyone that I showed my results to. It only annoyed me more, seeing that no one cared enough.

We made our way back to the apartment, complete silence throughout the streets. I said goodbye to Elizabeth and her dad and went upstairs to my floor. I took my slip and keys out from my pocket and unlocked the door. It was totally dark inside as none of the lights were on, and the only thing I could hear was quiet snoring.

My brother and dad had fallen asleep watching TV on the couch in the living room. I peeked into all of the rooms and saw everyone was still asleep. It felt wrong to wake them up, as they don't get many days to rest.

"Natalie?" I heard someone whisper from the living room.

"Dad?" I turned on a small lamp and saw that he had woken up.

"Hi, how was it? What'd you get?"

"Just look," I handed him the paper ball and sat down on the couch next to him.

7

"Oh, no…," he said, unfolding and reading the paper, "Really? The same as the rest of us? It's horrible what they do, but I can't say I didn't expect it. They totally lie to us."

"Exactly, everyone knows it's unfair, so why does nothing ever happen? Everyone just goes to work like they tell them to!"

"Well, I'm sure you know about all the people who randomly disappear and come back different. Those are the people who try to change things, that's why everyone's so afraid all the time."

"It's not worth it, you'll just end up in a worse place than where you were," I heard my mom say. I looked over and saw her walking out of her room. "It's not all bad, it's better than some of the other jobs they give out. What did Elizabeth get?"

"The same, Factory B," I said.

"See? At least you guys will get to work together. It's just how it is."

I took my paper and got up from the couch. It was frustrating that everyone was just accepting the results so I went to my own room and loudly closed the door behind me.

My room could only fit a metal bed with a mattress, a small wooden desk, a trash can, a candle holder, and a rack for the small amount of clothing I had. I sat on my hard mattress and crumpled the paper back up and threw it into the trash can. I wanted to burn it with the candle, but I was afraid that would cause a fire. There was nothing else to do, so I got into bed under my thin blanket. I tried closing my eyes and thinking about something exciting to fall asleep, but my mind kept going back to the job. I eventually felt myself slowly falling asleep to the light noise of the upstairs neighbor's footsteps.

I could tell it was late evening when I woke up because it was pitch black, although the house was still silent. I got up and went to the dark kitchen, lighting a match to illuminate the room. The light from the lopsided fridge blinded me, but when I looked inside, there were only a few ingredients.

I decided to eat some wheat bread and sat down on the couch in front of the TV. My dad and brother were now in their own rooms, so I skipped through the channels to try and find something interesting. An interview from inside the City caught my attention as I turned the volume slightly up.

They were outside on the sidewalk, chatter from people eating in the fancy cafes behind them. The interviewer wore huge diamond earrings and a necklace with a turquoise gem in the center. She had a royal red blazer and beige trousers, holding the microphone up to a girl who looked around my age and was wearing similar statement jewelry.

"So, we know the selection Ceremony was today, how do you feel?" The interviewer asked.

"Amazing, I got the perfect job for me! I can't wait for the first day tomorrow!" She answered with a huge smile.

"Great! Do you mind sharing with us what you got? Up to you."

"Of course! I got project manager for the City's tech development department! I start shadowing tomorrow."

I was working for the same company as her, but had a totally different job, working in the factory to make the parts for the department. I was too annoyed to watch the rest of the interview, so I shut the TV off. While my whole family would have to go to work with dangerous materials the next day, she would be able to spend her day in a comfortable glass building with air conditioning. I angrily turned the TV off and went back to bed.

My grandma woke me up early the next morning to get ready for my first day of work. My uniform was dropped off at our front door sometime during the night. It was a dark gray jumpsuit with pockets and looked slightly used. When I put it on, I realized it was too big, but I still had to wear it. I went to the kitchen where my family was eating breakfast. Although there was a plate for me, I didn't really feel like eating. I sat down in front of my plate anyway.

"How are you feeling about your first day? Nervous?" my dad asked.

"I already know I'm going to hate it," I said, crossing my arms.

"It's not that bad. You're going with Elizabeth, right?" my grandpa asked.

"It is that bad. I can't believe you guys are doing this. I have to do this same job for the rest of my life!"

"You'll get used to it and make new friends," my mom said.

"Stop trying to make it sound better!" I shouted, getting out of my seat.

The whole table was silent as I marched back to my room and slammed the door. I already felt exhausted before the day had even begun. I laid back in my bed and stared up at the ceiling, imagining the days of the people living in the City. I imagined them having a big feast for breakfast in a skyscraper, wearing expensive clothing, and driving to work in a limousine.

I thought about the girl from the interview the previous night. Even though I hated her, it was only out of jealousy. That motivated me enough to get myself out of bed and brush my hair with a prickly brush that had a few missing bristles. There was a knock on my door, signaling it was time to go. I grabbed my black boots and put them on. My family waited silently for me, and I could tell they were upset. We walked down the rusty stairs out of the apartment and onto the polluted street. The air was so bad that I had to put up my face mask. The only noise was from the fierce wind growing between buildings, blowing sand in my face and muting anything my family tried to say to me.

We finally got to the entrance of the factory where there was a small line to get in. Everyone needed to show their badge to security before they could enter, and I went into a separate line from my family to pick up my nametag. I met Elizabeth in line and cut to her spot.

At the front, they checked our names off from a clipboard and gave us our new name tags and badges. I stuck the name tag onto my uniform and put the badge safely in my pocket. The attendant told us our station number and we entered the inside of the factory. It was even bigger than I had thought, rows and rows of machines and workers stretching across the room. The air was musty and heavy, and I could see particles of dust floating in the rays of light. It smelled like metal and grease everywhere. I tried to say something to Elizabeth, but the loud sounds of sawing, whirring, and coughing covered it.

We finally got to our assigned row and found our letter. We were right next to each other, and there was a person next to each of us. Our job for now was to assemble the microchips. Once I was done assembling one, I would put it on the conveyor belt in front of my station. I wondered how anyone could do this for such a long time every day of their life.

I had assembled so many chips that I had lost track, when two people caught my attention. I only noticed them because they were the only well dressed and put together people in the whole factory, both wearing spotless white outfits. I only recognized one, the girl from the TV the other night. The person next to her was a man with a clipboard pointing out places around the factory to her. I turned to the person working next to me.

"Hey, what's her name?" I asked, nodding over at the two.

"I think the girl's name is Sasha. I heard her family is very important, she's probably here on a tour right now," the woman said.

"That's not fair at all!"

"Maybe not. What's your name?"

"Natalie. What's yours?"

"Mabel. Are you new here? I've never seen you before."

"Yeah, I got assigned yesterday. How long have you been here?"

"A real long time, about 40 years now."

"Really? How do you do it? I'm already tired on my first day."

"I felt the same way in the beginning, but it becomes part of your routine."

"Do you ever want a different job, though?"

"Sometimes, but I'm so used to being here. My work isn't too hard, it's mostly the air. It gets hard to breathe sometimes and it's very easy to get sick."

"Yeah, I've sneezed a lot from the dust."

"It'll stop after a while."

We stopped our conversation short for lunch break, which was in groups of rows. The lunchroom was rows of rusty wooden bench tables. Me and Elizabeth stood in line for the lunch, which I was nervous for. Lunch was potato soup, bread, and broccoli. We filled our trays and went to find a seat. The seats were filling up quickly as everyone went to go sit with their regular group. None of my family was in our lunch block, so we ended up sitting at a table that had 2 empty seats.

The tables each had 6 seats and at our table were 4 other people who all looked around 30 or 40 years old. They were busy talking with each other, so I turned to Elizabeth.

"So, how do you like it so far?" I asked.

"It's so boring. It's like the same thing over and over again, and it's only lunch time."

"I know! It literally feels like nothing happens here, everyone just does their work, no complaining."

"I don't believe it; they have to be drugging them or something."

"I wonder if anything interesting goes on here. Do you think there's ever been a protest?"

"Probably not, everyone's like a robot. There's also a lot of guards."

"I'm gonna ask," I said.

I turned around and saw that the other group at the table had finished their conversation.

"Hi, everyone! It's me and my friend's first day here. We're really surprised that we haven't seen or heard about something like a protest here yet. Would you guys know of anything like that happening here?" I asked, looking at the group.

"I hope you guys are having a good first day. There are stories of things like that in the past and every once in a while, you hear about someone trying something. But those things never go anywhere..." said the man next to me, nervously poking at his food and checking his surroundings.

"Well, why not?" I asked, curious.

"I don't know if we should be talking about this right now," the man said.

"Please? It's our first day here, we don't know anything," I argued.

"Look, we don't know much either. Usually, it's always one person who tries for one day and then gives up. Last time, the protest guy came back to work the next day totally different. He never mentioned an idea like that again. Honestly, I don't know what they do, but it's weird. We're not really supposed to talk about it, though," the woman next to him said.

"If you're thinking about trying it, I wouldn't recommend it. It's not worth it, nothing successful has ever happened in like 60 years," another man added.

"Wait, what do you mean the guy came back different?" I asked, thinking back to what my dad had told me the day before.

"I mean, I heard it was like he was a whole different person. He barely ever talked about his past after that. There are just a few rumors, but nobody can really talk about it. It's not important anyway, our point is that it isn't worth it to protest, you'll have a hard time finding people to join you," the woman whispered, quickly turning around when she locked eyes with a guard.

"Okay, thank you guys," I said, shifting back to face Elizabeth. "Do you think what they're saying is true?" I asked Elizabeth quietly.

"I mean, that's a weird thing to make up. What they're saying about protests is probably true, too. If you're thinking about it, I think you should think about what they're saying. It's been 60 years since anything good has come out of it."

"I was just thinking. I just want to ask a few more people, just for information. I want to know what people here think."

"Fine," Elizabeth said, finishing her food.

We didn't talk about work for the rest of lunch, and it was soon time to head back to our stations. On the way back, I had the chance to ask two more people who were walking together. They looked a little younger than the group before, but basically had the same answers. Everyone gave the same amount of information, always careful not to overshare. They seemed to agree that the protests were a bad idea, and nobody seemed willing to join.

I finished up my day assembling parts while talking to Elizabeth. Throughout the day, I noticed that many different guards took turns with their shifts and the workers were rarely alone. At the end, we signed out of work and walked back towards the apartment. I still wasn't ready to talk to my family, but I knew I would have to.

When I entered the apartment, everyone was gathered around the kitchen and setting the table for dinner. I was surprised to see that no one had greeted me. I kicked off my boots and immediately went to my room to change out of the greasy uniform. I changed into my night clothes and peaked out of the door.

It seemed like dinner was all ready and I saw there was food set in front of my chair. I walked to the kitchen and sat in my seat.

"So, how was your first day at work, Natalie?" my grandpa asked, breaking the silence.

"I hate it already."

"Well, you're going to hate it forever if you think like that," my mom said.

"I *am* going to hate it forever. If our whole family works in that factory, we'll never move out of this apartment or breathe clean air. We can't all stay sick forever."

"Be grateful for what you already have. If you stick to your job, you never know what could happen," my mom said.

"Nothing's ever going to happen! Barely anything happens there, you should know!" I exclaimed.

"It's because not enough people see the truth," my grandpa said, "they're all robots now."

"Exactly, I just don't understand why everyone continues to go to work, it's not like they all like it," I agreed.

"You've seen it now, there's security everywhere," my dad said.

"There *are* more workers than security though," my grandpa said.

"Let's stop talking about this now," my mom said, staring up at me.

I silently finished dinner and went back to my room. I could hear my family at the dinner table, continuing to argue. I lay in my bed, falling asleep to the sound of their voices.

Still annoyed, I woke up the next morning at the same time and got ready for another day. I wore another uniform that was the same as the first, and the same shoes I had worn the day before. On our walk to the factory, I saw Elizabeth and sped up to walk with her.

The entire walk there, I complained to Elizabeth about work and my family. She didn't say much but nodded in response to what I was saying. We signed in at the front and started walking back to our stations. I continued talking to Elizabeth until I couldn't hear my own voice over the sound of the saws.

As I passed by the other stations, I was shocked to see that all the workers looked expressionless. They didn't have any headphones or earphones, gloves, goggles, or any other protection gear. They were wearing the same clothes as us while working with the most sharp and loud equipment that I had ever seen. I recognized a girl that I had seen only a few days ago at the selection Ceremony, who already had a cast on her foot.

I was too shocked to finish my story with Elizabeth as we got to our station. After hours of repetitive work, we finally got to speak at lunch.

"Did you see the stations with all the saws presses? They didn't have any safety equipment at all! And did you see that girl from the ceremony with the cast?" I asked.

"I know, I saw! Why don't they give them any protection? Someone could actually die working at that station!" Elizabeth said.

"I can't even believe it. It only just made me want to protest more. Didn't you?"

"Actually, it just made me more grateful about the station that we have. At least we don't have to work with crazy machines like that. I mean, our job seems way better now."

"But that could've been you. Did you see how many kids at the Ceremony got factory job E? That's that place we just saw."

"I know, I feel so bad for them, but there's nothing much to do," Elizabeth said, looking down.

"Maybe."

We went back to our stations after lunch and continued our work, but I could only focus on the conditions of the factory. I hadn't noticed before, but it was filled with the sounds of coughing. The air quality inside was worse than anything I'd ever seen, an orange fog always covering everything. I saw that a worker next to me had brought his own mask from home.

After work, we all silently walked back to our apartment building, and I said goodbye to Elizabeth. I changed out of my uniform and went to the sink to wash it. During dinner, I wasn't paying attention to what my family was saying, because all I could hear were the coughs and the sniffles between each sentence. I wondered how many more days of working it would be before I started getting sick as well. My mind was already spaced out, so I decided to go to bed early.

I went through the same routine the next morning and we were out of the house before I knew it. Today was especially dusty so I pulled on my mask. We checked in and headed back to our station. I had decided to wear a different pair of shoes, and they were slightly too small so they kept digging into the back of my ankle.

After an hour of uncomfortable work, Elizabeth and I decided to go to the bathroom, which we had never been to before. The lady next to us gave us directions to the only bathroom in the building, and we started walking. While walking, we discovered parts of the factory we had never seen before. Some people were working with huge machines and others were carefully working on small vials of chemicals.

As I turned to talk to Elizabeth, I heard a loud, high-pitched scream. We quickly turned around to see someone had knocked over and broke a vial with a bright pink chemical inside. The chemical had spilled straight onto the arm of the worker.

We froze as we saw a nearby worker quickly hand her a wet towel to wipe it off, but it had already damaged her arm. She continued panicking, her arm red and bubbling.

I looked up when I heard a loud gasp. It was the same girl from the TV touring again with the same guide. The guide adjusted his glasses and quickly steered her away from the sight.

"Come on, Sasha. Let's move onto the next section," he said.

I saw the girl continue looking back as they quietly left.

We stayed frozen as a nurse quickly came and escorted the worker away, her crying eventually disappearing. To my complete disbelief, the factory went right back to normal. It was another minute before me and Elizabeth could walk away.

As we got back from the bathroom, all we could talk about was how everyone seemed so normal afterwards.

"Are you talking about the girl with the chemical burn just now?" the woman next to us asked.

"Yeah, that was insane. How did they all just move on that quickly?" I asked.

"It happens all the time here. Sometimes it's way worse than that."

"What? And nobody says anything?" Elizabeth asked.

"I think there were some protests a long time ago but nothing big recently."

"Why don't they?" I asked.

"They never really go anywhere. Anyone who helps organize one leaves for a few days and comes back really different," the woman whispered.

I wondered what everyone meant when they said different. There were always rumors when I was younger about what happened, but they all seemed exaggerated.

I went home thinking of all the possibilities of what had happened to the protesters. I wanted to ask my family about it at dinner, but clearly, they didn't like it when I talked about work or protests.

That night, I quickly got some leftover cardboard from our storage closet and dark markers from the kitchen. I lit the small candle and began writing messages on the cardboard. I traced over the letters carefully to make them more visible. I heard someone walking to the kitchen, so I blew out the light and safely stored the cardboard signs under my bed. Every time I tried closing my eyes, my nerves forced me to stay awake.

The next morning, I woke up early to hide my signs. I stuffed them in a dark brown backpack and put a sweatshirt on top of them just in case.

While we were walking to the factory, I saw Elizabeth ahead of us and quickly ran to her.

"Hi, what's with the backpack?" she asked.

"Look, I made this last night."

"No one is safe…The selection is a lie…," she read, "What is this?"

"The posters I made last night. I mean, there's just no way we're going back to work after yesterday. Come on, join me."

"Are you serious? It's way too soon, there's not enough people yet! Did you even really think about it?" she whispered, throwing her arms up.

"People are clearly too scared to join. We don't need anyone else; we can do it ourselves. Please join me," I begged.

"You should at least wait a few days, try to get some more people to join you!"

We stopped as we had reached the front of the factory and people were lined up to get in.

"Are you coming?" I asked, stepping to the side.

Elizabeth sighed loudly and rolled her eyes as she stepped to the side with me. I smiled and handed her a poster with BOYCOTT THE FACTORY in big red letters.

We waited for our parents to check in and go inside. Right in front of the entrance of the factory, I held up the sign high above my head. Nearby workers standing in the line turned to each other and whispered. I was hoping that some people would join, but they didn't. They stayed waiting in line and stared at us like we were strange.

All of a sudden, I saw a familiar face walking towards us from the line. As she came closer, I recognized her as Mabel, the woman who worked next to us.

"You guys need to go inside now before anything serious happens," she said.

"Why? We can't, we just started," I said.

"I've been working here a long time and I've already seen this happen before. It's better for everyone that you stop early on," she said, her face fully serious.

"Maybe it would be better if people actually joined us instead of just staring," I said loudly.

"But I know they won't join, so come inside now," she said firmly.

"I can't, I've already made up my mind," I said.

"Just trust me, this isn't going to work like you think it is."

"Thank you, but we'll go inside in a bit," Elizabeth said.

"I'm telling you, the sooner the better," she said, turning around.

More people walked by, some people nodding and some looking away. The line got shorter as people checked in and went inside. I looked at Elizabeth, who had her sign at her knees. I had also propped up the remaining posters on my backpack.

Before we knew it, there was no more line outside the factory. The wind blew hard in our faces, but I kept the sign held high. We turned around when we heard the main entrance open. Two guards fully dressed in uniform came out.

"Are they coming towards us?" Elizabeth asked quietly.

"Just keep holding it up," I said nervously.

Instead of coming closer, the guard on the left took out a small megaphone.

"You have 3 minutes to discard the signs and come inside before you permanently lose your jobs," they went back inside and the door shut with a loud thump.

"That's not a very big threat," I said.

"Come on, let's go. Everyone already saw the signs, there's nothing more," Elizabeth said, putting her sign down.

"You can go inside now, but I have to stay. I just can't work here anymore."

"Come with me! What's the point of staying out here?"

"There's no point in going inside for me. I honestly wouldn't work in there anyway."

"We don't have enough time for this, it's too risky to stay out here right now," Elizabeth said, pulling on my sign.

"I just can't go, but I'll see you after work?" I said, pulling back.

"Fine, but stay safe," she took her stuff and went back inside.

I was shivering from the wind when the two guards came back outside. I turned and pretended not to notice them as they approached me, but I was worried.

When I finally turned around, I felt a hard whack in the back of my head. There was an immediate throbbing before I quickly blacked out.

The next time I opened my eyes, I was almost blinded by the brightness. I could feel myself moving in a fast transport and pinched myself to wake myself up. I realized that I was on the train to the City, the one that I had always imagined myself being on. The section that I was in was completely empty. The only sound that I heard was the quiet buzzing from the train. I looked out the window to see we were moving across a small lake, heading towards the City.

Although I tried to keep my eyes open, my eyelids felt weirdly heavy, and my head felt groggy. I blacked out again to the sight of the City approaching.

I awoke again to the feeling of being pushed in a seat. This time, I was so tired that I could only squint my eyes. I felt like I was half asleep and half awake, and when I looked down, I noticed that I was in a wheelchair. I tried tilting my head up to squint at my surroundings, but I couldn't see much. All I could see was the almost painfully shiny interior of a building, and the last thing that I could make out was a doctor in a blue uniform opening the door for me.

I woke up to someone knocking on my door. I sat up and tried to open my eyes, but my eyelids were too heavy and my eyebags were so deep they were painful. My back and shoulders ached, maybe from sleeping wrong the night before.

"I know you're tired, but you have to get ready for work," my grandma whispered from the door.

I groaned and got up from my bed. When I stood up, the world felt like it was spinning away from me, and I painfully fell to the side. I looked at my outfit in surprise as I was still in my dirty work uniform. I tried to remember the night before and why I hadn't changed when I got home, but my mind was so foggy I could barely think. I slowly walked to the closet and put on a clean uniform.

When I finally left my room to go to the bathroom, I saw my family eating together in the kitchen.

"Natalie, how are you feeling?" my mom asked.

"Exhausted, I really don't want to go to work today," I said.

The whole table looked at each other weirdly, so I just walked away to the bathroom.

I brushed my teeth and combed my hair in the dark because the lighting felt too bright. The back pain and grogginess slowly went away but they were replaced by a painful headache. I felt like I could feel my heartbeat in my head. I was too tired and didn't have enough time for breakfast, so we left right after I came out of the bathroom.

"Do I really have to go to work today? My head hurts," I asked as I put on my shoes.

"Just try to go today. You can't miss any more days," my dad said.

"Any more days? When have I ever not gone?" I asked, confused.

"What he meant is that you should try to go whenever you can to save up your rest days, right?" my grandma said quickly.

My dad nodded and they all hurried out of the house. I didn't really pay attention to what they were saying as I was still trying to recall the night before.

As we slowly walked to the factory, I felt a tap on my shoulder and turned around to see Elizabeth.

"Hi, Natalie! It's good to see you! How do you feel?" she asked.

"Weird, like I feel foggy and my head hurts so bad I can barely think."

"Really? What do you mean by foggy?"

"I don't know, like it's hard to concentrate kind of. I can't explain it."

"What's the last thing you remember? Like, before you woke up?"

"I think it's because my head hurts right now, but I can't remember anything after going home from work last night."

"Last night?"

"I mean, yeah. Why?"

"Wait, so….," she lowered her voice, looking around, "you don't remember that protest we did? Or that whole day?"

"What protest? What day?" I whispered.

"This is strange…" she said as we reached the factory.

"I don't remember any protests. The last thing I remember is that day we saw that girl get the chemical burn on her arm. I remember going home that day and then my memory weirdly trails off," I said.

"We have to be quiet, so they don't listen in. There was a day after that where we had this whole protest. You really don't remember that?"

"No, I'm trying, but I don't," I whispered, moving up in the line.

"Let me tell you what I remember…"

Elizabeth recalled the whole day of protest and how when she left work that day, she didn't see me. I didn't remember anything she was saying, and we were both left totally confused. We spent the rest of the day trying to figure out what had happened after Elizabeth had gone inside. My brain was still mixed up so it was hard for me to concentrate.

The speakers rang loudly, signaling it was the end of the day. We walked out together, still trying to piece together the story.

"How is it possible to forget an entire day? And you said I was sleeping for 2 days straight?" I asked, signing out at the front.

"Yeah, it's too weird. The guards must have done something, but I don't know what. Your head feels weird, right?" Elizabeth asked.

Before I could answer, someone from behind us tapped my shoulder. We turned around to see the girl from the TV who I'd kept seeing around the factory.

"Hey, come with me really quick," she whispered. She turned around and walked to an area near the dumpsters, away from the crowd. We followed.

"Who are you?" Elizabeth asked, looking around nervously.

"My name is Sasha; I work for corporate at this company. I overheard you guys talking and I think I recognize you," she said, pointing at me.

"Me? From where?" I asked.

"You're the girl who was protesting outside, right?" she asked.

"I mean, yeah, but weirdly I don't remember it," I answered.

"I think I know why, my family was talking about it at dinner last night," she continued. "They were saying how there was a girl outside of our factory who was protesting with a bunch of signs a few days ago. They said that even after a warning she didn't go inside, so they had to take her to the medical center in the City."

"Medical center? To do what?" Elizabeth asked.

"At the medical center, they wipe people's memories. It's been happening for a long time, before any of us were born," she said.

"So that's why I can't remember the past few days!" I exclaimed loudly.

"Shh! Yeah, and it's also why your head hurts," Sasha said.

"If it's been happening for a long time, why does no one talk about it?" I asked.

"You're not allowed to talk about it, they usually threaten the families. It's this big secret. People know something happens, but most of them don't know what it is," she answered.

"How often does it happen?" Elizabeth asked.

"It doesn't happen that much anymore. They only do it when people organize a protest or something, but that hasn't happened in a really long time. Apparently, there were some problems last time they wiped peoples' memories, but they've improved it a lot."

"What problems?" I asked.

"Some people got their memory back, and there were a lot of rumors about the wiping," she answered.

"But won't you get in a lot of trouble if you tell us this?" Elizabeth asked.

"It's fine, they won't find out," she replied, "I have to go now."

"Well, thanks for telling us," I said.

"Yeah, thanks! It makes a bit more sense now," Elizabeth said.

"No problem, bye!" She turned around and went back into the factory.

"Woah, what are we gonna do now?" Elizabeth asked.

"I don't know, but we should go home first. I need to think about this when my head doesn't feel so weird."

We quickly rushed home and agreed to meet the next day to discuss. After dinner, I still couldn't stop thinking about what Sasha had said. I wanted to speak with my parents about it, but I knew they wouldn't want to discuss it at all. So, I quietly went into my grandparents' room when I saw the light in my parent's room switch off.

"Hi, Natalie. What's going on? It's late already," my grandma asked.

"I just wanted to talk to you guys about something," I answered.

"What is it?" my grandpa asked.

"Well, I've been feeling really weird the whole day and after work some girl came up to us. She told me and Elizabeth that she knows that my memory was wiped after I was protesting. Is that true?"

My grandparents looked at each other and sighed.

"Look, we've really been wanting to tell you, but they threatened us not to, and we didn't want to cause more trouble. Who's the girl?" my grandma asked.

"Sasha. Her family owns the factory we work at. She was also saying how there hasn't been any memory wiping or protesting for a long time. I can't believe me and Elizabeth were the only ones in such a long time!"

They looked at each other again, before my grandma nodded.

"Well, we were actually there at that time when there was a lot of protesting. We had just started working at the factory, like you, and we wanted to join in. Back then, there were a lot more people protesting and they were having a hard time controlling it," my grandpa said, lowering his voice.

"So, then what happened? Why did they stop?" I asked.

"They started wiping everyone's memories, and it happened to us too. But the technology was different back then, so our memory eventually came back," my grandma continued.

"Yes, so some people went back to protesting until one of the leaders of the protest back then was shot by one of the guards at a protest. They threatened all the other leaders and told them that anyone else who continued to protest would also be killed. After that, all the protesting stopped and nobody spoke about it. Nobody was allowed to talk about the wiping either. Soon, everything went back to normal and even now people are still too scared to protest," my grandpa said.

"What? I can't believe I never knew about that. How can they keep such a big thing a secret?" I asked.

"A lot of people, especially people there at the time, actually know about it. It's just never talked about," my grandma whispered.

"If I just get more people to know everything that the government actually does, I think I can get enough people to help me protest successfully," I said.

"I know you want to, but it's just not a good idea right now. It won't work with the way things are unfortunately," my grandma warned.

"But then it'll never be the right time!" "You heard what happened to the last leader, it's too dangerous. Especially with all the new technology they have now, you don't know what to expect," my grandpa added, "We should all go to bed now, it's already late."

"I guess," I sighed, "good night."

"Good night!" they whispered back as I left the room.

As I left, I already knew I couldn't keep going back to work.

On our walk to the factory the next morning, I looked around for Elizabeth and quickly spotted her as I got in line for the entrance.

"Hi, Elizabeth!" I said, tapping her shoulder.

"Oh, hi! I'm so tired from last night, I couldn't really fall asleep," she said, yawning.

"Yeah, same. I just kept thinking about what that Sasha girl said. It's scary that they've been doing that for so long and we just now found out!"

"I know! How's your head feeling?"

"Actually a lot better, and a lot of the brain fog is gone too. I wanted to talk to you and Sasha, but do you think she's here today?" I asked, moving forward.

"Maybe…we can check the office. I know that some of the corporate people work in the office at the factory a couple days in the week."

"Okay, smart. We can go check once we're inside."

During lunch, we went to visit the office instead of the cafeteria. We peeked inside the window and saw a few different people sitting at desks, typing on keyboards. We spotted Sasha sitting at a seat close to the window and started waving, trying to get her attention. We almost decided to head back when she finally got up to throw away a paper and spotted us. She looked around the room quickly before leaving.

"Hi, guys! What are you doing here?" she asked.

"Well, I wanted to talk to you both about something my grandparents said. Last night, I was telling them about the stuff you told us yesterday, and they said that they were at the protests a long time ago that you mentioned. They had their memory wiped too, but like you said, it came back. They said that the reason the protests stopped back then was because one of the leaders got shot and then people were threatened. But it seems like they were able to get a lot of people out to the protests."

"Someone died? That's scary, I didn't even know that part!" Sasha responded.

"Me neither, I guess they did a good job at hiding it," Elizabeth said.

"I think that if we plan this right, we can get a lot of people to show up to the protests now, too," I said.

31

"No way, you just said that the last leader got killed!" said Elizabeth.

"We could do it secretly, so they don't know that we're leading it," I responded.

"But how would we do it secretly?" Sasha asked, curious.

"Well, we would definitely need evidence of this first. I just don't know where or how we would get it," I answered.

"If there's any documents, they're probably stored in the same building as where they wipe the memories," Sasha said slowly.

"You mean all the way in the City? We can't get there, we're not allowed on the train without permission," I said.

"Don't worry about that, I can help you guys get into the City and the building. But once we're there, we would have to look quickly."

"But I don't understand...why would you help us?" Elizabeth asked slowly.

Now that I thought of it, Sasha didn't have anything to gain from helping us. If she got caught, she would get caught in the mess and end up in a world of trouble.

"Ok, you can't tell anyone this," she said, lowering her voice, "but my dad actually used to work at the same factory here apparently. I was never able to meet him because my mom's family never approved of their marriage, so he had to move away. My mom's family owns the factory, so they have a lot of power. A few years ago, I overheard them saying that he had passed away from a lung disease. I never knew what the disease was from until I came to work here, and now I know it had to be from the air quality in these factories. I see everyone getting sick."

"I'm sorry, I can definitely understand. Most of my family is also sick from working here, but they don't try to fix the conditions. They barely give people time off!" I responded, and Elizabeth nodded.

"I agree, I just wished they cared enough to make the factory quality better," Elizabeth added on.

"Exactly, and I think I know how to get you guys into the City. There's a truck that takes the materials from the factory all the way to the building in the City every other day," Sasha said.

We spent the rest of the lunch break quietly planning out how to break into the building and get out safely without getting caught. We then agreed to meet at the same office right after checking into work the next morning as the alarms rang, signaling the end of the break.

I had lots of concerns about our plans, but I wasn't worried about Sasha deceiving us. We finished the rest of our day quietly, too nervous to talk about our plans out loud. As I got home, I had no intention of telling anyone in my family about the plan. I knew that if I told even my grandparents, they would tell my parents, and we would never be able to go through with it.

I went to bed with a huge pit in my stomach. I knew that if we got caught sneaking into the City, we could be in a lot more trouble than the protest.

I woke up early the next morning and put on the same uniform, knowing I wasn't going to work at all. As the rest of my family got ready, I quickly snuck up to the roof. The sky was particularly clear today, and I could see the City well. This was going to be my second time there, but I couldn't remember anything about it. I couldn't admire it for long, because my family was leaving for the factory. I ran downstairs in time to take my empty bag and walk out with my family.

When I saw Elizabeth, all I asked her was if she was ready. She nodded but she had a concerned look on her face. We signed in at the front, but instead of following the crowd to our station, we slipped off to the office. When we got there, Sasha was already standing in front of the door and had an equally nervous look on her face, while holding two empty shipment boxes.

"So, you guys remember the plan, right? I asked Manny, the shipment guy, yesterday on his way out, and he agreed to let me come along. We have to hurry and get there before he does."

We nodded and followed her out to the loading dock. There was only one shipment in the morning, so we easily saw the truck. The boxes were already laid out next to the truck, ready to be loaded in. Sasha pressed a button to open the cargo door and unfolded the 2 big shipment boxes she brought, setting them up in the very back corner of the container truck. Elizabeth and I took two of the actual shipments and hid them behind a dumpster on the side of the building. We quickly climbed into the back of the truck, and I realized how much space there actually was inside. Elizabeth got in her box first, and we lightly taped up the top of her box. I stepped back to make sure it looked realistic. It looked like any other box, but there were actually tiny holes poked through everywhere and there was a giant hole on the side facing the wall, making it breathable.

"How do you feel, Elizabeth?" I whispered.

"It's actually not too bad, does it look okay?" she asked.

"It's perfect," I said, getting into the box next to hers.

Sasha quickly taped the top of my box and the light shined in from the tiny holes. It was a bit uncomfortable since I had to cram inside it, but I was able to sit with my knees bent and it was easy to breathe because of the giant hole in the back.

I could hear Sasha loading more boxes into the truck to hide ours in the back. After a few minutes, I heard the delivery driver come out.

"Hey, Sasha. Are you already loading up the boxes?" He asked.

"Yeah, I got here early today so I thought I would try to get a head start."

I held my breath as I heard them finish loading up the rest of the boxes.

"You can get in, I'm just going to count them and make sure we have the right number of boxes," he said.

I could feel myself sweating as he slowly counted off the boxes, making his way to the back.

"20, 21..." he counted, tapping the top of my box.

He then left the shipment compartment, and I heard the door shut. We were completely silent on our ride there, but I could hear the sound of voices coming from the front seats of the truck. I was nervous that my foot would cramp up the whole time and it was a bit uncomfortable every time the truck went over a bump. It was completely dark in the box now and I could feel my back begin to hurt.

After a long drive, I felt the truck finally come to a stop. There was some talking in the front again, and then I heard them get out and walk towards the back. As the compartment door opened, I could finally hear their voices.

"Wow, that was a long drive," I heard Sasha say.

"I know right, I swear it takes way longer than the train," he responded.

"Wait, before you unload the boxes, can you show me where the bathroom is here?" She asked.

"Uh, sure," he said, as I heard their footsteps walk away.

The moment I felt they were far away enough, I pushed hard on the top of my box and opened it. I quickly stepped out, knowing we didn't have a lot of time. Next to me, Elizabeth got up as well.

"Let's go," I whispered.

We quietly got out of the truck and ran out of the shipment garage and into the janitorial closet right next to the door where we agreed to meet Sasha.

The closet was completely dark, and there wasn't a lot of space.

We waited another few minutes before we were blinded as the door opened. The lights in the building were unnecessarily bright.

"Sorry, that took so long, how are you guys?" Sasha asked.

"We're good, how long do we have?" I asked.

"He said he's leaving in about 20 minutes, so we need to move quickly."

Luckily on Thursdays, the workers in the building had a late start so it was empty, but Sasha warned us that some people may come in early. All the doors required an access badge, which Sasha luckily had. We took the elevator up to the 5th floor and Sasha got out first to make sure no one was in the hallway. We then quickly got out and found the storage room. "Remember, try to focus on finding the files with the names from the wiping," Sasha said, locking the door from the inside.

We got to work trying to find the documents, opening up every file cabinet and drawer we could see. The building seemed to be some sort of research building that performed all kinds of operations and experiments. Each file was packed with information, so I tried my best to skim only the front of each.

The room was quiet except for the sound of cabinets opening and closing. I began to read the files so quickly I wondered if I had accidentally missed it.

"Five minutes until we have to get back," Sasha reported, checking her watch.

"I think it's this!" Elizabeth exclaimed, holding up a red file.

We all crowded around Elizabeth and flipped through it. Each page was stamped with the official government heading and the pages were organized into columns. Each column stated a name, a date, and WIPE next to it. To verify that it was the right document, I flipped all the way to the back and found my name on the last row.

"This is it! We can look at the details later, but we have to go right now," Sasha said, closing the file cabinet.

I grabbed the file, and we quickly ran out of the storage room. We took the elevator down and ran to the garage, hoping that we had made it before Manny had. Sasha quietly opened the door and confirmed that he wasn't there yet. We opened up the back of the truck and got in. This time, there were no more boxes, and we had the whole compartment to ourselves. Just as the cargo door closed, we heard the garage door open. Soon after, we felt the engine start.

As the truck pulled out of the garage, I realized that the cargo compartment was bumpier than I had thought, and we had to sit leaning against the wall to keep balanced.

I tried to read through the files, but it was almost pitch-black inside the compartment. I had almost fallen asleep to the sound of music from the front when I felt a huge jolt. The truck had driven over a big bump, and we were sent sliding across the container, crashing into the back wall with a loud thump.

"What was that noise? I thought I emptied out all the boxes," I heard the driver say from the front.

"What noise? I didn't hear anything," Sasha responded.

"No, I definitely heard something in the back. If I didn't empty out all the shipments, we'd have to turn back," he said.

Although we tried to be as quiet as possible, I felt the truck pull over to the side.

"I feel like this is really unnecessary. We need to be back to the factory soon," I heard Sasha say.

"It'll just take a second," he said, opening his door.

Elizabeth and I looked for places to hide, but the truck was completely empty. I heard Sasha's door opening as well before we were blinded by the cargo door opening.

The driver looked at us confused and Sasha walked up next to him with an upset look on her face.

"Woah…who are you guys? How did you get into the truck?" He asked, slowly turning to Sasha.

I struggled for a moment, trying to find an excuse. There were seconds of silence and staring at each other before I recognized his uniform. It looked like it was from the same factory that our uniform was from. I soon realized that the driver probably was from the same town.

"Wait, just read this!" I exclaimed, holding out the file.

He took the file and flipped through it.

"What is this? What's wiped?"

"The government's been wiping people's memories! I had mine wiped recently. We were just trying to get proof," I explained, panicked.

"I don't know… I think I have to report this," he said, slowly handing me the file again.

"Wait! You work at the factory too, right? Your uniform is like ours," Elizabeth said.

"Do you really want to work there forever? We're trying to help everyone," I added on.

"I'm sorry, I can't get caught helping you guys," he responded.

"If you don't say anything, no one will ever find out," Sasha said, "my family owns the factory, and I'll make sure that your name never gets mentioned."

He stood silent for a moment, trying to figure out what to do.

"Fine, I won't say anything but just make sure none of this ever gets out."

We thanked him as the door shut again.

The remaining drive was short, but I no longer heard music or conversation from the front. The truck pulled into the driveway and stopped. Elizabeth opened the door, and we quickly got out, slipping back into the factory.

"There's like an hour left before the day ends. I can stay after everyone leaves the office and print out copies of the document, but I don't think I can help post them up. If I'm not back by dinner, it'll be too suspicious. There's a late train so after

I print them out, I can leave them somewhere for you guys," Sasha said.

"How about at the mailbox in front of town hall? They only use it for voting, so I don't think there'll be anything else in there, right?" I asked.

"Yeah, that sounds good," Elizabeth agreed.

"Okay, I'll print them out and leave them there. We should all get back, we've been gone for really long," Sasha said as we reached the office.

"Okay, thanks for everything!" We said.

"Sure, good luck guys!" She smiled before she went inside.

We subtly returned to our station and got back to work. "Where were you guys? You know I had to cover for you twice," Mabel, the woman working next to us, asked.

"My head has been hurting a lot the past few days, so we just went to visit the medical center," I quickly said.

"What did they ask?" Elizabeth asked.

"They just asked where you guys were, and I said you were in the bathroom. You didn't tell them that you left?" She asked.

"No, we knew they would say to go after work," I said.

"Oh, well, alright," she answered, returning to work.

I exchanged a nervous look with Elizabeth. I knew that Mabel wouldn't tell the guards, but I was afraid she would tell someone who would.

We ended work without any more problems and began walking home.

"So, what time do you think we should meet tonight? It's got to be in the middle of the night when everyone's sleeping, right?" I asked.

"Definitely…I think by 2 should be fine. I think the latest shifts end by 12 tonight, so by then it should definitely be all cleared out," Elizabeth responded.

"That sounds good. Are you gonna try and get some sleep before?" I asked.

"I don't know if I can. The alarm clock is in my parent's room and it's way too loud to be ringing at 2 am."

"Me neither, I think I'd be too nervous to fall asleep anyway."

"True, there's a lot of ways it could go wrong. Like, what if Sasha couldn't deliver them? Or a guard catches us, or someone hears us?"

"We just have to be as quiet as possible, and if anything goes wrong, we can just try again another day. The good thing is that there's no money for cameras around this town."

"Yeah, I just hope I accidentally don't fall asleep," Elizabeth said, walking up the stairs.

"Yeah, and not wake up anyone when I'm leaving either," I said, reaching my floor.

"Well, I'll see you at 2!" Elizabeth waved.

I waved back and went inside. I shivered as it got cold easily at night during this time of year. After dinner, I checked the time to see that it was only a bit past 8. As everyone went back to their rooms, I stayed in the living room and watched TV.

Our TV was small and randomly turned off at times. I flipped through the channels, which went up to 20, and found an interesting documentary on animals. There were no animals in our town as it was an industry city with basically no nature. The only time I had seen real animals was on the TV and in the zoo a long time ago. I turned down the volume all the way to not wake anyone up and watched the entire thing, fascinated. After I was done, I continued flipping through channels and even silently cleaned my room. By the time that I was done also cleaning the kitchen, it was finally 1:45.

I went back to my room and put on a warm outfit. Even though I knew there were no cameras, I put on a cotton mask to be safe. I then quietly went to the kitchen and got out rolls of tape and put them in a backpack. I made sure to wear my lightest boots and slowly left the house, closing the door. I walked downstairs to the first floor. I waited at the front door until I heard Elizabeth quietly coming down the stairs. She also had on a mask and carried a backpack.

We silently speed walked to the town hall, getting hit by hard gusts of wind. Many of the streets were narrowly packed between buildings and the wind was always the strongest there.

We finally made it to the town square, which looked strange when it was completely empty. Besides one bright lamp on the entrance of the town hall and a few dim lights on the surrounding buildings, it was very dark.

"I hope it's in here," I whispered, opening up the mailbox.

I sighed with relief as I pulled out a thick stack of papers, each a copy of a page from the files we had gotten. I split the stack in half and gave the other to Elizabeth.

I took a moment to look through the papers. I scanned the lines and saw 2 names that I knew very well.

"Look, it's my grandparents," I whispered, showing Elizabeth.

"That's crazy, I still can't believe the same thing happened with them!" she quietly answered.

We took out the rolls of tape and began taping them up around town. I went up to town hall first, making sure to cover the entrance with the papers. I then went around to the other buildings, most of which were old apartments. I was still shivering from the cold as the papers in the stack became thinner. I looked back at Elizabeth, who was posting them up on the other side of the square.

I posted up the last of my papers on our medical center. The center was too small and run-down to be very helpful, so most people only went for minor injuries. If someone needed real help, they would have to pay a lot to go to a doctor in the City, so most people tried to deal with their problems themselves, including my family.

I walked over to Elizabeth who had finished putting up her flyers as well. She pointed nervously at a window in the apartment building right in front of us. One of the windows was open and a light was on inside the room.

"We should go now," she whispered.

We speed walked out of the town square and back to our complex. As we got farther away from the square, the buildings began to look worse. Closer to the square were the more expensive apartments, which weren't very nice either. Some of the buildings there even had small lobbies and the rooms had windows. They were also the only apartments that were taller than 6 floors and had elevators, though they were very slow.

Our apartments were farther away from the square, but they weren't the worst in town. The only really bad thing was that there were no windows, and it could get suffocatingly stuffy inside.

"I'm happy that's over," Elizabeth said as we finally got to our   apartment. "Me too, and now I can finally go to sleep. It's hard to even stay awake right now."

"I know, too bad we have to go to work tomorrow," she replied.

"Maybe not, hopefully the signs actually do something," I said.

"Yeah, you never know how they'll react I guess," she responded.

We waved goodbye as I tried opening my door as quietly as possible. When I entered, I was relieved to see all the lights off. I slowly snuck into my room as my eyes adjusted to the complete darkness inside. I closed the door and finally felt some relief. I quickly changed and got into bed, imagining all the ways people would react the next day as I fell asleep.

When my grandma woke me up the next morning, it felt no different than a regular day. I still got up to eat the same food and change into the same outfit. It was only as we finally left the apartment when I felt the difference. The reason we had posted the papers up around the town square was that basically everyone had to walk through that area on their way to work in the morning, but it was causing some traffic. The crowds moved slowly as people looked around confused.

"We're already late, what is up with the crowds this morning?" my mom asked, checking her watch.

As we got closer to the square, people began to stop to read the signs. I quickly lost my family in the crowds and instead got distracted by people's reactions.

I felt a tap on my shoulders as I was listening in on a family's conversation about the flyers.

"Oh my gosh, hey!" I turned around to see Elizabeth and Sasha.

"Hi Natalie, isn't this crazy? The square's totally full!" Sasha exclaimed.

"The factory is probably empty right now, they're too busy reading the flyers," Elizabeth said excitedly.

We walked around the square, listening in on people's conversations and seeing all the different expressions people had. Some people even had the flyers in their hand, trying to get a closer look.

"That's my mom's name right there!" We heard one boy yell.

I knew that the flyers had gotten their attention, but I didn't know what the next step was.

We leaned in on a conversation between some workers I recognized from the factory.

"I wonder who did all this. How did they even get the documents? I mean, they have to be real, look at the stamps!"

"Yeah, there's no way someone can fake that."

"Who cares who did it? What happens now? Are we all just supposed to go back to work?"

"The officers will probably be here soon from the City. If someone says something now, people might finally listen!"

That was something we kept hearing as we walked through the crowds. They kept mentioning how they wished someone would step up so things would be different, but no one was actually doing it.

"Why can't someone else finally do something? We've basically done everything," Elizabeth whispered, annoyed.

"All the evidence is right there," Sasha agreed.

I thought back to what Elizabeth had told me about our protest, and how everyone in line refused to even look at us.

"I think we just need to do one more thing. We should organize a town meeting for tonight quietly, since we know no one else will," I whispered.

"How do we even do that quietly?" Sasha asked.

"Just go around and tell people that you heard about the meeting from someone else. That way it's not risky at all," I said.

"Where would we have the meeting, though?" Elizabeth asked.

"What about the factory? It's completely empty at night and huge inside," I asked.

"Yeah, and a lot of people are already familiar with it," Sasha added on.

"How are we going to get inside tonight? I know they lock all the doors," Elizabeth asked.

"I'll stay after everyone leaves and let you guys in after they lock it. I can just tell my parents I'm spending the night at a friend's house since it's Friday," Sasha said.

"Really? That's perfect! When do they usually lock the doors?" I asked.

"By 8 all the guards are gone, and the doors are locked."

"Ok, so how about we set the meeting for 10 tonight, at the factory?" Elizabeth asked.

"Okay, let's try to tell as many people as we can," I said.

We walked around the square, loudly talking about the meeting at night. Some people stopped their conversations to listen in.

"The meeting at 10 in the factory? That's late, but I'll definitely be there," I repeated loudly.

At one point we separated, going around to join conversations and spread the word.

I went up to a group I recognized from the factory. "So, are you guys going to be there tonight?" I asked.

"Be where tonight?" A girl asked, confused.

"Wait, you didn't hear yet? Some other girl told me that there's a town meeting at 10 at the factory tonight about the flyers."
"Oh, really? Well, are you going?" Another boy asked.

"I mean it's late, but I have to. It sounds really important, and I don't want to miss out," I answered.

I continued having similar conversations with multiple groups, telling people I had never seen before. I was telling a woman who worked at the medical center when I heard some guards yelling into a megaphone in front of town hall to get people moving.

I finished telling her the details as the crowd slowly started to go their own ways, but I knew that I had told enough people.

I followed the crowd and slowly began walking towards the factory. I spotted Elizabeth and Sasha ahead of me and ran up to them.

"How was it? Do you think you told a lot of people?" I asked quietly.

"I hope so, I basically went up to everyone," Elizabeth replied.

"I think I did too, but I think some people were suspicious of me," Sasha said.

Even though she wasn't wearing any expensive jewelry, her uniform was different from our uniform and easily stood out.

We finally followed the crowd up to the factory and went inside. As we passed by the different stations, we saw that instead of working, lots of people were huddled in groups and whispering.

"Hi, Mabel! Did you see those signs around the square?" I asked when we got to our station.

"Yes, I even recognized a few names on the papers!"

"Well, did you hear about the secret meeting tonight?" I lowered my voice.

"The one here tonight? Some kids told me about it in the line."

"Oh, good. Are you going?" I asked.

"Yes, I think so! Are you two?"

"Yeah, we'll see you there tonight!" I said.

I continued telling as many people as I could, many of whom had already heard about the meeting from someone else.

Before we left work, Elizabeth and I went to find Sasha. We looked through the office window but didn't see her inside. Just as we were about to leave, Elizabeth spotted Sasha leaving the bathroom.

"Hi, guys! Are you ready for tonight?" She asked.

"Definitely, it's gonna be huge. A ton of people I asked are coming."
"So you're going to open the doors for us before 10, right?" Elizabeth asked.

"Yep, right after the guards leave. I'm going to hide out in the bathroom until they finish clearing the building."

"Ok, great! We'll see you then!" We waved goodbye and quickly left.

When I got back to my apartment, my parents were already making dinner. As we sat around the table, I kept waiting for someone to mention the posters or the meeting. I was shocked when the dinner ended without a word about it. I never told my parents about the meeting because I knew that they would never go to a meeting like that, and if they knew, they would try to stop me from going.

I went back to my room and waited for the time to hit 9:30, as we had planned to get there a bit earlier than 10. When it was finally time, I changed back into a warm outfit and packed another mask just in case.

As I was putting on my boots at the door, I heard lots of commotion coming from the other rooms. A second later, the rest of my family came out of their rooms, fully dressed.

"What are you doing Natalie?" My mom asked, shocked.

"Well, I'm going to the meeting at the factory, what are you guys doing?" I replied slowly.

"Us too…" she answered.

We stared at each other in surprise for a few seconds. I had automatically assumed that they would never go to a secret meeting, but it turned out that even they were going.

"We better hurry, then! We can't be late," I said, tying my laces.

"I don't know if you should be going," my dad said.

"You know I'm going to go anyway."

My whole family, except my brother, met up with Elizabeth's family and began walking towards the factory quietly.

"Wow, honestly, I didn't expect them to be coming," Elizabeth whispered to me.

"Me neither, but I guess that just means the whole town's going," I replied.

As we got closer, the crowd started to get bigger. Everyone was silent, not wanting to alert anyone who wasn't supposed to know. The crowd stopped moving as the people in the front had reached the factory and they seemed surprised to find out the doors were unlocked.

I held the door for the people behind me and looked inside. The factory looked strange when there weren't people working everywhere. Someone had lit candles inside and placed them all around.

We rushed past the crowd, looking for Sasha. We finally found her in a corner, lighting a candle.

"Did you light all those candles?" We asked.

"Yeah, after the guards left I realized it was pitch dark in here. I had at least an hour before you guys came so I found these candles and lit them."

"It looks so good! Doesn't it feel so weird to be here without working?" Elizabeth asked.

"Definitely, I think it feels more peaceful," she replied.

We joined the crowd in the middle of the factory, where there was a large open space. It was so full that people had started taking places farther away, some sitting on tables and factory belts.

"This has to be most of the town, right?" I asked.

Before they could answer, I heard a familiar voice speak up. I looked up to see Mabel standing on top of a table, getting people's attention.

"We all saw the posters this morning! There's no way we can continue going to work anymore! The whole town has to strike!" Mabel yelled.

The factory was filled with murmurs and applause as people looked around for the next person to speak up.

"Starting tomorrow, no one goes to work!" Someone else yelled out.

"We need to get this to other towns, I'm sure the same thing happens over there," a man I had never seen before added.

"I have driver friends from other towns, I can let them know!" A familiar looking man next to us said. When I looked closer, I realized that he was the truck driver from earlier.

"Look guys, it's Manny!" Sasha whispered excitedly.

As more people began adding on, I realized that this was going even farther than I had expected.

"We should form a picket line tomorrow around this factory! Don't go to your usual workplace, just come here in the morning!" Another man exclaimed.

"Is 9 okay with everyone?" Mabel called out.

There was a loud murmur of agreement and people nodded their heads.

"Okay, then! Tomorrow at 9, instead of going to work, come to this factory instead! Come prepared with posters and masks!" Mabel repeated loudly

"Try to get the word out to people from other towns, too!" Manny added.

The factory filled with applause and chatter as people began discussing the new plan. People began calling out their ideas for posters and giving tips.

The woman speaking was interrupted when there was a loud noise at the front door. People began yelling and scrambling different ways as a group of guards loudly barged into the factory, throwing smoke bombs into the crowd. We quickly got off of the table and began running with a group to the side entrance.

We ran outside into the cold dark and hid behind the dumpsters where we had first met Sasha, laughing loudly.

"How do you think they found out?" I asked between laughs.

"I guess someone ratted at the last moment! They're way too late now, though!" Sasha answered.

"I definitely hope they don't find out it's us!" Elizabeth laughed.

"I'm just glad I don't have to go to work tomorrow…" I said.

"Me too, but I'll still have to keep coming to this town to see you guys! My parents probably won't want me working here after this," Sasha said.

"Thank you for helping us out, I can't believe that you did all of that for us and you don't even work in the factory!" I said.

"It's no problem, I would never be able to work here knowing all the stuff that happens. You guys should come visit my house some time! I can sneak you around the City," Sasha said.

"I would love that!" Elizabeth exclaimed.

"Me too, I've always wanted to actually visit and look around," I said.

"There's so many things to do!"

Before we could say anything else, we heard guards coming around the corner and sprinted away from the dumpsters. As we separated in the crowd, I began looking for my family, concerned that they hadn't made it out of the factory. I ran towards the direction of our apartment when I was pulled to the side into a random alley.

I turned around nervously before seeing that it was my family.

"We've been looking for you! Where were you?" My dad asked.

"I was just saying bye to Sasha and Elizabeth! Is everyone here?" I asked. I squinted into the dark alley to see my grandparents smiling and waving at me.

"Sasha? Who's Sasha?" My mom asked.

"I'll explain it later, it's a very long story. Don't be mad, but first, I need you guys to know that it was us who put up the flyers and stole all the documents..." I said.

"Of course, we already knew that," my parents laughed.

We slipped back into the crowds and began running home again. Although I was running through the chaos of the crowd, I felt a strange sense of relief. I hadn't realized it before, but all the secrets and sneaking around had been wearing me out. As I looked around at the full crowd of runners, I felt overwhelming hope for what would come next.

About the Author

Madison Park is a high school student who enjoys writing all kinds of genres. Outside of writing, Madison enjoys going on hikes and painting.

www.ingramcontent.com/pod-product-compliance
Lightning Source LLC
Chambersburg PA
CBHW021938170626
46807CB00007B/3179